# 20,000 Leagues Under THE SEA

## Jules Verne

# Artist: Li Sidong

First edition for North America (including Canada and Mexico),
Philippine Islands, and Puerto Rico published in 2009
by Barron's Educational Series, Inc.

*All inquiries should be addressed to*:
Barron's Educational Series, Inc.
250 Wireless Boulevard
Hauppauge, NY 11788
**www.barronseduc.com**

ISBN-13 (Hardcover): 978-0-7641-6246-6
ISBN-10 (Hardcover): 0-7641-6246-2
ISBN-13 (Paperback): 978-0-7641-4279-6
ISBN-10 (Paperback): 0-7641-4279-8

Library of Congress Control No.: 2009927377

Picture credits:
p. 40 © Print Collector/HIP/TopFoto.co.uk
Every effort has been made to trace copyright holders. The Salariya Book Company apologizes
for any omissions and would be pleased, in such cases, to add an acknowledgement in future editions.

Printed and bound in China
9 8 7 6 5 4 3 2 1

# 20,000 Leagues Under THE SEA

## Jules Verne

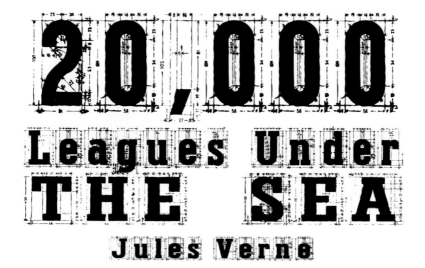

*Illustrated by*

Li Sidong

BARRON'S

*Retold by*

Jacqueline Morley

*Series created and designed by*

David Salariya

The sea is everything! It covers seven tenths of the earth. Its breath is pure and wholesome. It is an immense desert where man is never alone, for he feels life pulsating all around him. The sea is the living infinite: the means through which man may lead an almost supernatural existence. It is all movement and love.

*Captain Nemo*

# CHARACTERS

Captain Nemo
inventor and captain of the *Nautilus*

Pierre Arronax
professor of marine biology

Ned Land
a Canadian whaler

Conseil
Professor Aronnax's manservant

Commander Farragut
captain of the USS
*Abraham Lincoln*

The *Nautilus*

# THE SEA UNICORN

In the spring of 1867, I, Professor Pierre Aronnax, was in New York completing a lecture tour when my attention was caught by the headlines being shouted everywhere.

*Sea monster strikes again!*

A mysterious sea creature was threatening shipping around the world. Much larger than a whale, it could move at incredible speed and spout jets of water 50 meters high. As a marine biologist,[1] I was keenly interested.

Experts worldwide were arguing over it. Clearly, it could not be man-made.

*An underwater vessel of such size and speed? There is no power capable of driving it![2]*

Whatever it was, the thing was dangerous. It had rammed a transatlantic liner packed with passengers and holed her below the waterline.

Lives were at risk; maritime[3] trade was imperilled. Action was demanded in the US Congress.

*The sea must be purged[4] of this dread cetacean,[5] at all costs, once and for all.*

Journalists pestered me for my opinion as an expert. I told them there was only one sea creature with a tusk that could bore such holes.

*The monster must be some giant form of the narwhal[6] — the sea unicorn.*

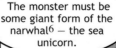

1. marine biologist: a scientist who studies sea life.
2. no power capable of driving it: Submarines did exist in the 1860s (a few were used in the Civil War), but they were very small and were powered only by men turning handles.
3. maritime: sea-going.     4. purged: cleared.     5. cetacean: whale, or whale-like animal.
6. narwhal: a type of whale, usually no more than six yards long. Male narwhals have a single long, straight tusk.

# THE HUNT FOR THE MONSTER

The next sighting was in the North Pacific. A high-speed frigate,[1] the *Abraham Lincoln*, was equipped to hunt the monster. The mission was entrusted to Commander Farragut.[2]

On the eve[3] of my return to France, I received a cable.[4]

> The US Government would be pleased for you to represent France in this enterprise.

Without a moment's hesitation I called my trusty manservant, Conseil.

> Get my things ready. We leave in two hours.

> Whatever monsieur[5] wishes.

Thousands of well-wishers lined the piers as we left New York harbor. By nightfall we were heading full steam into the Atlantic.

The ship had the most up-to-date artillery[6]...

...and another weapon: famous Canadian harpooner Ned Land.

Ned and I were soon good friends, though we disagreed about the monster.

> You can't tell me a narwhal could hole an iron ship.

> A giant narwhal is far from impossible.

We headed south for several weeks, traveled around Cape Horn[7] and entered the Pacific at last. Now everyone was on the lookout. The rigging[8] was alive with sailors.

> Twenty thousand dollars to the man who spots it first!

---

1. frigate: a fast, medium-sized warship.   2. Commander Farragut: The name of this character is taken from the real-life Admiral David G. Farragut, a hero of the American Civil War.   3. eve: the day before.   4. cable: a telegram – an express message sent along an electric wire.   5. monsieur: French for 'Sir'; it also means 'Mister' when placed before a person's name.   6. artillery: heavy guns.   7. Cape Horn: the southern tip of South America.   8. rigging: ropes and chains used to support sails and masts.

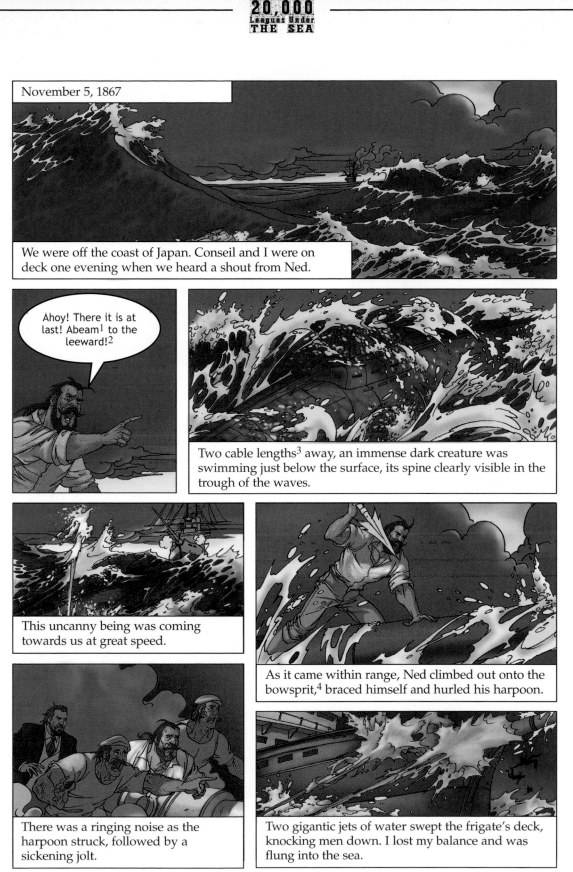

November 5, 1867

We were off the coast of Japan. Conseil and I were on deck one evening when we heard a shout from Ned.

Ahoy! There it is at last! Abeam[1] to the leeward![2]

Two cable lengths[3] away, an immense dark creature was swimming just below the surface, its spine clearly visible in the trough of the waves.

This uncanny being was coming towards us at great speed.

As it came within range, Ned climbed out onto the bowsprit,[4] braced himself and hurled his harpoon.

There was a ringing noise as the harpoon struck, followed by a sickening jolt.

Two gigantic jets of water swept the frigate's deck, knocking men down. I lost my balance and was flung into the sea.

1. abeam: directly to the right or left of the ship.
2. leeward: the side of the ship that is facing away from the wind.
3. two cable lengths: 1,200 feet (366 meters).
4. bowsprit: a strong pole that projects from the bow (the front end) of a sailing ship.

# PRISONERS!

I plunged under the water and rose gasping. I was starting to panic when I realized I was not alone.

Conseil! You were thrown in, too!

No — but I'm in monsieur's service so I had to follow him.

The *Abraham Lincoln* was disappearing in the distance. Why wasn't she looking for us?

Her steering's gone. The monster got her rudder and propeller.

Then we're lost!

After two hours we were numb with exhaustion. But, just as the sea closed over my head, I bumped into something solid.

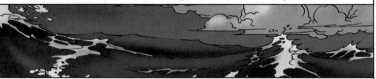

I found myself lying on a hard surface, looking into the faces of Ned Land and Conseil.

This is your so-called narwhal! It's made of steel!

We were on some sort of narrow floating island. Ned had been thrown onto it by the collision.

A hatch flew open; the crew of the machine leapt out and pulled us inside.

We were locked in a cell. The door soon reopened and a man, evidently the captain, stood there. He studied us keenly as I explained our plight.[1]

He made no answer, but gave orders in some strange tongue and we were locked in again.

After two hours Ned's fury was at a boiling point. When some crewmen entered, he leapt at them.

1. plight: dangerous situation.

The intimidating figure of the captain was again in the doorway.

Stop, Master Land! And you, Professor, listen to me!

I should put you back on deck, order my ship to dive and forget you existed.

I am not what you call a civilized man. I have rejected society,[1] for reasons of which I am the judge.

You do not speak like a civilized man.

Since our vessel had attacked his, he was treating us as enemies.

We could stay on board, the captain said, on one condition. There might be future happenings we must not witness. He did not like to use force, so at such times we must agree to return voluntarily to our cell.

Do you accept this condition?

We accept. But I would like to ask how soon we shall be able to leave this vessel.

You have stumbled on a secret that no one must know.

Never!

So you are merely giving us the choice between life and death!

To me, the sea is everything! On land they can impose their unjust laws, fight and devour[4] each other...

... but here I have no master. Here I am free!

The captain invited me to lunch. I asked how I should address him.

To you, I am just Captain Nemo.[2]

To me, you are just passengers aboard my ship, the *Nautilus*.[3]

Now, if you would like to inspect the *Nautilus*, you are welcome.

1. society: the company of other people.
2. Nemo: Latin for "nobody."
3. *Nautilus*: The ship is named after a kind of shellfish which lives in a spiral shell divided into separate chambers.
4. devour: eat up, destroy.

# THE *NAUTILUS*

We passed through the captain's library into a large hall containing valuable paintings. There was an organ at one end, and cases along the walls held a priceless collection of rare objects from the sea: coral, fish, plants, and fantastic shells.

> What an opportunity for advancing my studies!

The captain's cabin was very plain. There were scientific instruments on the walls.

> The manometer measures our depth and the water pressure on the vessel.

I wanted to know what powered the *Nautilus* – what provided its heat, light, and motion.

> Electricity![1]

> Responsive,[2] quick, and easy to use!

I was surprised. I had heard that scientists were exploring the possibilities of electric power, but, as far as I was aware, its batteries had a very feeble output.

> I have devised a powerful battery using sodium extracted from the sea.

> That is our dinghy.

> We use it for fishing and excursions.

I noticed, amidships,[3] a compartment on deck resembling an upturned boat.

Finally we came to the engine room.

> In this section electricity is generated.

---

1. Electricity!: Electrical power was a new and exciting idea at this time. German engineer Werner von Siemens built the first industrial generator in 1866. Electric motors that work the same way as modern ones were not built until the 1870s.
2. responsive: easy to control.
3. amidships: in the middle of the ship.

How had the captain built this vessel in total secrecy?

Each part was ordered from a different country, using a different name.

We assembled them on a deserted island and destroyed all trace of our work.

The cost must have been staggering. You must be very rich.

Very, very, rich, monsieur. Fabulously rich.

Sliding panels in the walls were now drawn back, revealing huge windows. Ned and Conseil were stunned.

Where are we? It looks like a fancy hotel!

As the *Nautilus* submerged, its searchlight revealed a dazzling underwater world. Countless species of fish swam within an arm's length of us. I was entranced.

Not so Ned. He could not bear inaction. To him the glass was like a prison wall.

I begged him to calm down and see how things developed.

This is like being in an aquarium.

Except that in an aquarium the fish are captive. Here they are as free as birds.

# THE FORESTS OF CRESPO

One morning I received a note from the captain.

> Captain Nemo invites Professor Aronnax and his friends to a hunting party in the forests of Crespo.

> A chance to escape!

But when Ned learned that these were underwater forests and he must put on diving gear, he refused to come.

> I'm not wearing one of those!

Conseil and I were given diving suits, air tanks, and watertight guns powered by compressed air. We entered a special chamber. Its door was sealed behind us and the room began to fill with water. It rose over our heads until the whole chamber was filled.

An outer door opened and we stepped into the sea. The smooth sand was lit by sunlight filtering from above. Walking was easy; the water supported me and I barely felt the weight of my suit.

> Beautiful! Beautiful!

Opal-tinted jellyfish floated over our heads. If only I could have expressed my joy to Conseil! But our helmets made speech impossible.

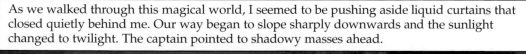

As we walked through this magical world, I seemed to be pushing aside liquid curtains that closed quietly behind me. Our way began to slope sharply downwards and the sunlight changed to twilight. The captain pointed to shadowy masses ahead.

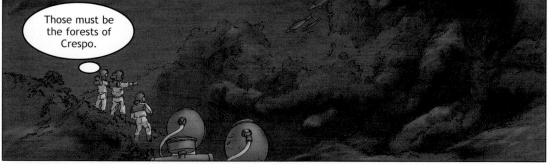

Those must be the forests of Crespo.

We entered a forest of large, tree-like seaweeds, carpeted with sea anemones and other flower-like animals.

At noon the captain gave the signal to halt. We had been walking for four hours and I was glad to rest.

I lay down, but something made me sit up suddenly. I was being watched! An enormous sea spider was about to leap on me. I was grateful to the crewman who dispatched it[1] with his gun.

What other fearsome creatures lurk here?

The captain shot a magnificent sea otter.

1. dispatched it: killed it.

# PARADISE ISLAND

New Year's Day, 1868

We passed from the Pacific into the Indian Ocean through the Torres Strait, one of the most dangerous waters in the world.

Its countless rocks and islets[1] make it almost impossible to navigate.

This captain had better know his course, or the coral could smash the hull to pieces.

A sudden jolt threw me backwards. The *Nautilus* had struck a reef!

Has there been an accident?

Not an accident, monsieur, merely an incident.

But Captain Nemo did not seem at all worried.

In five days we shall have full moon.

Five days stuck here! Let's explore the islands!

I shall expect that obliging satellite[2] to lift us off.

Don't waste your fire on parrots. They're no good to eat.

Amazingly, the captain let us go, and Ned rowed us to the nearest island. Ned was desperate to eat fresh meat for a change.

Ned shot a wild pig, so he got his evening grill.

What do you say we don't go back this evening?

We were feasting and planning the next day's trip when a stone fell in our midst.

We saw men armed with bows and slings running towards us.

Back to the boat!

1. islets: small islands.
2. that obliging satellite: the moon. "Obliging" means "helpful"; a satellite is any object which orbits around a larger object, such as the moon orbiting the earth. Nemo knows that tides are caused by the pull of the moon's gravity. At full moon the rise of the tide will be higher than usual (because at that time the moon and sun are in line and the sun's gravity pulls in the same direction as the moon's), and the water will be deep enough to float the *Nautilus* off the coral.

Ned rowed with all his might. A hundred or so angry islanders were pursuing us in canoes.

I found the captain in the saloon, playing the organ, totally absorbed in his music.

I was dumbfounded by the captain's unconcern.

A score of islanders scrambled on deck.

When we open the hatch to take in air, they'll get in, too.

Professor, are these islanders worse than anyone else?

Let them try. I do not want my visit to cost them a single life.

But as soon as they touched the rail they were thrown back by an invisible force.

Ned rushed out to see what was happening.

Our attackers beat a hasty retreat[1] while we consoled the unfortunate Ned. The tide lifted the *Nautilus* from her coral bed at the exact day, hour, and minute that the captain had predicted.

When he grasped the rail, he was thrown back too.

A thousand devils! I've been struck by lightning!

The captain had a secret weapon: he had run an electric current through the rail.

We left the Torres Strait safe and sound.

1. beat a hasty retreat: to run away.

# THE CORAL CEMETERY

January 18, 1868: the Indian Ocean. The sea was rough; a storm was coming.

I found the captain studying the horizon with his spyglass.[1] Something disturbed him.

He gave an order to his lieutenant in their strange language, and the *Nautilus* picked up speed.

Intrigued[2], I fetched my own telescope and put it to my eye.

It was violently snatched from me by Captain Nemo!

The captain's eyes lit up menacingly; his whole body was possessed with hatred. But it was not I who had aroused his fury – it was something on the horizon.

I must ask you to observe the conditions of our bargain.

You and your companions must be confined until I choose to release you.

Well, at least lunch is served!

Within minutes the captain had regained his usual calm. He turned to me with a commanding look.

Four crew members marched us to the cell in which we'd spent our first night. You can imagine Ned's rage.

Imprisoning wasn't enough; he's drugged us too. Whatever he's hiding, it can't be good!

After eating, Ned lost no time in falling asleep, and to my surprise so did Conseil. I too felt myself overcome by drowsiness.

1. spyglass: telescope.
2. intrigued: interested, curious

1. haggard: tired and worried.
2. quarters: living space on a ship.

# THE PEARL DIVER

January 28, 1868

We were now off the west coast of Ceylon.[1] The affair of the wounded man had altered my idea of the captain. He no longer seemed an idealist, shunning the corrupt world of men. That mysterious collision, his sudden fury, our drugging – all these suggested that he had a secret purpose, perhaps a violent one.

I was musing on this when the captain joined me.

Ceylon is famous for its pearl fisheries. Would you care to visit them?

Pearl divers have a short life; the work is dangerous and their pay is pitiful.

By the way, you're not afraid of sharks?

At dawn the dinghy ferried us to the offshore fisheries and we put on diving gear. But why did we not have lanterns?

Better not to use them. They might attract some dangerous residents.

Does he mean sharks?

We went beneath the waves.

Millions of oysters clung to the rock faces. We collected them eagerly.

Calling me over to a grotto,[2] the captain showed me a giant oyster enclosing an enormous pearl.

He would not let me touch it – he was cultivating it to be the centerpiece of his collection.

1. Ceylon: an island off the southern tip of India, now called Sri Lanka.
2. grotto: a small cave.

The captain gestured to us to hide.

A diver was at work, taking as many oysters as he could rip free in one breath.

Suddenly the diver made a desperate leap. As if from nowhere, a shark was bearing down on him! A blow from its tail flung him to the ocean floor.

Captain Nemo drove his knife into the beast, trying to reach its heart. As he stabbed repeatedly, it opened its jaws over him.

Ned, with the speed of lightning, hurled his harpoon. The shark's death spasms were horrendous.

We rushed the diver to the surface, where after some minutes he recovered. Captain Nemo gave his own bag of pearls to him.

By breakfast time we were back on the *Nautilus*.

You risked your life for that man, yet you despise all men.

That Indian lives in the land of the oppressed[1] — and so do I.

1. the oppressed: those who are exploited or treated unfairly by others. At this period, Ceylon and most of the Indian subcontinent were ruled by the British.

# THE ARABIAN TUNNEL

January 30, 1868: the Red Sea.

Where could the captain be taking us? He must have known that the Suez Canal was still unfinished.[1] He was heading for a dead end!

Ned fumed and wanted to know what the devil the captain was doing. We were stunned when he assured us that within two days we would be in the Mediterranean.

I know a channel, below sea level, that links the Red Sea with the Mediterranean. I have named it the Arabian Tunnel.

Certainly, monsieur. There need be no secrets between us — since we shall never part.

Impossible! We'd never sail around Africa in just two days.[2]

May I ask how you discovered it?

No need to try! We shall go *under* Suez.

The captain had noticed that the two seas had many types of fish in common. He had caught specimens in the Red Sea, ringed them[3] and thrown them back...

The captain invited me to the pilot house[4] while he negotiated the tunnel. The move was risky and he always took the wheel himself.

...and a few months later caught the very same fish in the Mediterranean!

Cautiously we entered the tunnel.

1. Suez Canal: a man-made waterway, opened in 1869, which runs across Egypt from the north end of the Red Sea to the Mediterranean Sea.   2. sail around Africa: Before the Suez Canal was built, the only route from the Red Sea to Europe was by sailing entirely around Africa.   3. ringed them: attached a metal ring to one of their fins so that they could be identified.   4. pilot house: steering cabin.

For a time we skirted an underwater wall of rock. Then a deep chasm appeared before us and the *Nautilus* plunged boldly in.

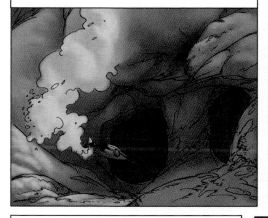

The waters made a strange rustling sound as we shot like an arrow down the sloping tunnel. The propellers were put into reverse to cut down our speed. Twenty minutes later we were in the Mediterranean.

When Ned woke next morning and realized where we were, he came to see me. His fierce look dismayed me.

Let's have a little chat, if you please.

We are in European waters now. Before this mad captain drags us to the poles and back, I suggest we jump ship.

I was not at all eager to leave, because of my studies. Through the *Nautilus* I was learning more about sea creatures every day. I played for time.

We may have a better chance later, nearer France or England, or even America.

You always talk of the future. If we near land I'm getting the dinghy out.

Secretly, I didn't think he'd get an opportunity. The captain did not trust us and was avoiding the coasts. So I made Ned a promise.

When the chance comes, Conseil and I will follow you.

# MILLIONS UNDER THE SEA

We were passing the island of Crete now. When I went to the saloon I found the captain pacing up and down, gloomy and preoccupied.

Suddenly, through the window I saw a man in the water.

There's a man there drowning! We must save him!

Don't worry about him.

It's Nicolas "the Fish," a fearless diver. He swims constantly between the Greek islands.

The captain opened a safe packed with gold ingots.[1] He filled a large chest with them.

He sealed the chest and wrote an address on it in Greek. Then he pressed a button and four men entered and carried out the chest.

Permit me to bid you goodnight.

That night I felt the *Nautilus* surfacing and heard the dinghy being launched.

Where did Nemo get the gold? To whom is he sending these millions?

I was still awake at dawn when the dinghy returned.

We shot across the Mediterranean at speed. The captain did not like being so close to the world of men. We were off the coast of Spain when Ned burst into my room one morning.

It's all set for this evening. We're not far from land. Nine o'clock at the dinghy. I've told Conseil.

1. ingots: bars or blocks of cast metal.

Alas for Ned's escape plans! That afternoon the *Nautilus* settled on the ocean bed. The captain came abruptly into the saloon and asked me a very odd question.

What do you know of Spanish history?

Not a great deal, I fear.

The captain gave me a history lesson. In 1702, Spanish galleons[1] loaded with gold and silver from the Americas were trapped in Vigo Bay by an English fleet.

To save such an immense treasure from the English, the Spanish admiral set his galleons on fire and sank them.

This may answer a question that has been puzzling you.

So this is the source of Nemo's enormous wealth.

There are thousands of needy people in the world, who could do with some of this wealth.

The sea floor was covered in gold, silver, coins, and jewels.

Captain Nemo turned on me angrily. He was clearly very offended.

What makes you think I do not make good use of it?

Do you think I am unaware that there are people in this world who are suffering, victims who are oppressed?

I realized he had given that chest of gold to the freedom fighters on the unhappy island of Crete.[2]

1. galleons: a heavy sailing ship used for war or commerce.
2. unhappy island of Crete: At this period, Crete was part of the Ottoman (Turkish) empire. Nemo supports those who want it to be part of Greece instead.

# ATLANTIS

February 19, 1868. The compass was far from reassuring: we were turning our backs on Europe and heading south-southwest, into open sea.

We're not finished yet. Next time we'll score a bull's-eye.[1]

Some evenings later the captain surprised me by coming to my cabin around 11 o'clock and asking, in the friendliest way, whether I was tired. I told him I was not.

In that case, would you care to make an interesting excursion in the dark?

Roads?

We'd have a long climb and the roads are bad.

The two of us set off alone in the inky darkness.

The captain headed towards a reddish glow in the distance. It was shining from behind a mountain a few miles off.

We began climbing steeply, through what seemed like a forest of trees without leaves or sap.

It was some time before I realized that these were real trees, now fossilized[2] under many fathoms[3] of water.

1. score a bull's-eye: achieve exactly what we want to do – that is, escape to dry land.
2. fossilized: turned to stone by a natural process over thousands or millions of years.
3. fathoms: a unit used by sailors to measure the depth of water. One fathom = 6 feet = 1.83 meters.

The supporting water made me fearless. I leapt across crevasses[1] whose depth would have made me shrink back on dry land.

We passed between rock faces pitted with black caves where the eyes of monstrous shelled creatures sparkled in the dark.

My blood froze whenever a huge antenna or snapping claw shot out across our path.

I was puzzled by rocks that seemed like paving slabs or even the remains of buildings, but the captain urged me on impatiently towards the summit of the underwater mountain.

We gained the peak[2] and gazed into the valley beyond.

At our feet, lit by fiery streams of lava from a belching volcano, lay a vast ruined city.

ATLANTIS! The fabled[3] city drowned by the sea! In my mind's eye I saw its gleaming marble temples, its theaters, palaces, and spacious harbor as they were on the day they vanished beneath a gigantic wave, 12,000 years ago.

They said it never existed, because no one could find it — no one but Nemo, and he has shared the secret with me!

1. crevasses: deep cracks in the sea bed.
2. gained the peak: reached the top.
3. fabled: legendary. According to the ancient Greek philosopher Plato, Atlantis was a mighty empire that suddenly sank into the sea, thousands of years ago.

# THE SECRET FACTORY

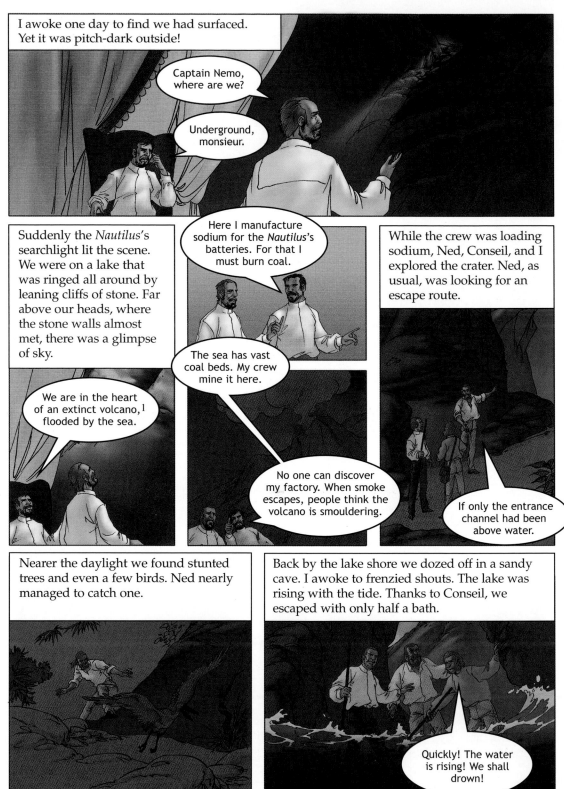

I awoke one day to find we had surfaced. Yet it was pitch-dark outside!

Captain Nemo, where are we?

Underground, monsieur.

Suddenly the *Nautilus*'s searchlight lit the scene. We were on a lake that was ringed all around by leaning cliffs of stone. Far above our heads, where the stone walls almost met, there was a glimpse of sky.

We are in the heart of an extinct volcano,[1] flooded by the sea.

Here I manufacture sodium for the *Nautilus*'s batteries. For that I must burn coal.

The sea has vast coal beds. My crew mine it here.

No one can discover my factory. When smoke escapes, people think the volcano is smouldering.

While the crew was loading sodium, Ned, Conseil, and I explored the crater. Ned, as usual, was looking for an escape route.

If only the entrance channel had been above water.

Nearer the daylight we found stunted trees and even a few birds. Ned nearly managed to catch one.

Back by the lake shore we dozed off in a sandy cave. I awoke to frenzied shouts. The lake was rising with the tide. Thanks to Conseil, we escaped with only half a bath.

Quickly! The water is rising! We shall drown!

1. extinct volcano: one that is not likely ever to erupt again.

March 14, 1868. We were now speeding into the south Atlantic. There could be no escape in that deserted sea. Ned was finding the monotony[1] of our life unbearable.

How many men do you think there are on board?

The *Nautilus* can store two days' air for 625 men. But I doubt there's a tenth of that number.

Hmm. That's still too many for the three of us to handle!

I advised Ned to be patient.

March 16: inside the Antarctic Circle.

Before long we were surrounded by icebergs.

Somehow Captain Nemo always found a way through.

SMASH!

But soon our way was barred by continuous ice. The *Nautilus* charged at it with frightful violence, breaking the brittle mass with a terrible cracking sound.

Two days later we were completely frozen in. Before us stretched endless chains of ice – the Great Ice Shelf that not even the bravest explorers had crossed.

Your captain may be superhuman, but he's not stronger than nature.

He'll have to stop now, like it or not!

How did the captain mean to get us out of this fix? Where was he heading next?

Further south.

South?!

Where others have failed, I will not fail.

Together we will discover the South Pole.[2]

Do you mean to give the *Nautilus* wings and fly over the ice?

Not over it, Professor, but under it.

1. monotony: sameness, lack of variety.
2. discover the South Pole: In 1868, nobody had ever been to the South Pole. In real life, it was first reached on December 14, 1911 by a Norwegian expedition led by Roald Amundsen.

# To the Pole and Back

Ice has a lower density than water, and rises to the surface; although the sea was iced over, its depths would not be frozen. The *Nautilus* would travel below the ice! I was thrilled. This was a great scientific project.

There is some danger in going several days without access to fresh air.

But the *Nautilus* has huge reserve tanks. Fill them up and we'll have all the air we need.

Utter madness!

The *Nautilus* was chipped free and plunged below the ice. We headed at speed straight for the Pole.

We were sometimes forced to extraordinary depths by the thickness of the ice above us.

March 19, 1868: The *Nautilus* surfaced into open sea and sunlight.

To find out whether we are at the Pole, we need to plot the sun's position at midday.

But by midday the sun was hidden in a bank of mist. It was the same the next day.

Tomorrow is our last chance.

The sun will not be visible for another six months.[1]

March 21: the crucial day. The sun was sinking in a clear sky.

If at noon the sun is exactly bisected[2] by the horizon, we shall know we are at the Pole.

The captain followed the sun with his telescope. I read the chronometer,[3] my heart pounding.

Noon!

The Pole!

On March 21, 1868, I, Captain Nemo, take possession of this part of the earth, an area equal to one-sixth of all known continents.[4]

In whose name, Captain?

Mine, sir!

1. another six months: at the Poles, during the polar night, the sun stays below the horizon for 179 days.
2. bisected: divided in half.     3. chronometer: a very accurate clock or watch.
4. all known continents: We now know that the South Pole is part of the continent of Antarctica. It is not in the open sea, as Verne imagined.

1. rising . . . through the water: Because ice is less dense than water, the capsized iceberg is bound to float back up to the surface. The *Nautilus* risks being crushed between the rising iceberg and the underside of the ice shelf under which the submarine has sailed.

# BREATHLESS

We were prisoners inside the ice shelf with only two days' supply of air! The captain called the crew and addressed us all.

> Gentlemen, in our position there are two ways of dying.

> The first is to be crushed to death, the second is to be asphyxiated.[1]

We had only 48 hours to cheat death. The captain proposed a drastic solution.

> We shall escape by cutting through the ice.

The ice below us was 30 feet thick. Working in relays, we began to hack at the ice non-stop.

We needed to cut a trench large enough to let the *Nautilus* drop through.

Ned, Conseil, and I worked alongside the crew. After each two-hour stint we returned exhausted.

> At this rate we need four days at least, not two.

Inside the *Nautilus* the air was getting foul. It could not be renewed; the diggers needed all our dwindling supply.

As we dug down, the sides of the trench grew inwards as new ice formed. The ceiling above us was getting lower too.

> We'll be sealed up in this water. It's solidifying like cement!

> It's hopeless. Even if we get through the iceberg, we'll still be under the surface ice — with no more air.

1. asphyxiated: suffocated.

Nemo had a desperate plan: to use the *Nautilus'* huge boilers that distilled[1] water for drinking.

We pumped all night, and by next day the temperature near the *Nautilus* was warm enough to soften the ice. Nemo gave orders for the *Nautilus* to be maneuvered to the bottom of the trench.

We'll pump boiling water out to melt the ice. In such an enclosed space it might work.

Then we'll fill all her water tanks at once. The increase in weight should send her crashing through.

Our lives depend on this final effort.

The valves were opened wide and 100 cubic meters[2] of water poured in, suddenly adding 100,000 kilograms[3] to the *Nautilus'* weight. The ice split and she fell through it.

It worked!

But we were still under the main ice shelf, without any new air. My face was purple, my lips blue. I felt death approaching.

A nightmare race began. We tore through the water at the terrifying speed of 40 knots.[4] The manometer showed we were now only 7 meters[5] below the surface and rising.

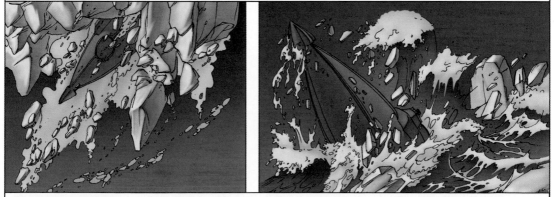

There was a tremendous jolt. We had rammed the crust of ice and broken through to the surface. The hatches opened and waves of fresh air flooded in.

1. distilled: The process of distilling water to remove salt and other impurities involves evaporating the water (boiling it into steam) and then condensing it (cooling it so that it returns to water).    2. 100 cubic meters: 131 cubic yards/3,530 cubic feet.    3. 100,000 kilograms: 220,500 lbs.    4. 40 knots: 46 miles per hour, or 74 kilometers per hour.    5. 7 meters: 23 feet.

# A Debt Repaid

From the Pole we headed north into the Atlantic. We had now travelled over 16,000 leagues,[1] and had been Nemo's prisoners for six months.

**Does this madman mean to take us to the North Pole, too?**

**I wouldn't put it past him!**

April 20, 1868: We were now in the warm waters of the Bahamas. Ned suddenly sprang towards the window. A giant squid was following us.

**What a hideous monster!**

The *Nautilus* came to a sudden stop. The squid had jammed the propeller. As Nemo opened the hatch to inspect the damage, a long tentacle slithered down the stairs. He severed it with one blow of his axe. The rest of us seized weapons and rushed on deck.

A tentacle snaked through the air and seized a crewman. To my dying day I shall remember his desperate cry.

**Help! Help! Help!**

As we fought to save him, the monster released a blinding jet of black ink. When the cloud cleared, squid and victim were gone.

Another squid had seized Ned. I sprang to help, but Nemo was quicker. He buried his axe in the creature's throat.

1. leagues: The league is an ancient unit of measurement equal to the distance a person can walk in one hour. One French league at this period equals 2.5 miles (4 kilometers.)

The captain shed tears for his dead crewman.

*You saved me from the shark. I have repaid the debt.*

Ned merely bent his head.

We were soon in the busy North Atlantic. Ned was always on the look-out for other ships – but to brave such seas in a dinghy meant certain death.

*I'm suffocating in this tin box! We're close to Canada, my homeland. I'll make him let me off!*

With Ned in this mood, I decided to appeal to the captain. He was working at his desk and was not pleased to be disturbed.

*I am writing an account of my life and discoveries.*

*On my death it will be sealed in a container and thrown into the sea.*

*I could take it to safety, if you would give us our liberty.*

*Your liberty?*

*Ned Land may do as he likes. I did not seek him out and I do not keep him here for my pleasure. I have no more to say.*

*Monsieur Aronnax, I repeat what I told you months ago.*

*Whoever enters the Nautilus must never leave her.*

*But think what the need for freedom might force a man like Land to do.*

The captain grew more and more silent and withdrawn.

A ferocious hurricane arose as we passed Long Island. The captain, roped to the deck, braved the storm all night, as if defying the elements.

# NEMO'S REVENGE

Ned, Conseil, and I were on deck when we saw a large vessel on the horizon.

If that ship comes within a mile of us, I'm jumping into the sea.

They're firing at us!

Can't they see there are men on board?

BOOM!

SPLASH!

I realized Ned had hit upon the truth. Since the clash with the *Abraham Lincoln*, the whole world knew the "monster" was a hostile submarine. Now every warship was after us.

Perhaps that's why they're firing at us.

Darn it! Let's signal. They'll know that some of us are decent men.

POW!

Ship of an accursed nation! I do not need to see your flag to know you, but I will show you mine.

Ned took out his handkerchief to wave, but was struck by a blow from an iron fist. It stretched him on the deck despite his strength.

Fool! Do you want me to nail you to the prow[1] when I ram that ship?

Captain, are you going to attack that ship?

1. prow: the pointed bow (front end) of a ship.

I am going to sink her, Professor.

Horrified, I consulted Ned and Conseil. We were all agreed: better to sink with the warship than stay and be this man's accomplices.[1] As soon as the ship was close enough we would jump into the water.

But suddenly we heard the familiar hissing sound of the *Nautilus* filling her tanks in order to submerge.

Too late! We're under water! He's going to ram her below the waterline.

There was a slight shock as the *Nautilus'* steel spur penetrated the ship's hull like a sailmaker's needle going through canvas.

My hair stood on end as the huge mass of the ship sank into the water. There was a sudden loud explosion.[2] The captain watched like a satanic judge, silent, cold, and implacable.[3]

Then, without a word he went to his cabin. I saw him gazing at a miniature[4] of a young woman and two children. His shoulders heaved with sobs.

1. accomplices: people who help to commit a crime, or who take no action to prevent a crime being committed.
2. explosion: As the water rushed in, it compressed the air inside the hull, which shattered the decks.
3. implacable: merciless.   4. miniature: a small painting or photograph, often in a fancy frame.

# THE LAST OF CAPTAIN NEMO

I now felt a horror of the captain; luckily, he seemed to be avoiding us. We were still heading north at speed. At dawn one day, waking from a nightmare about the sinking ship, I found Ned standing over me.

We haven't seen captain or crew for days. We're in sight of land.

I've got it planned: we escape tonight.

By now I was as eager as Ned to be free of our ruthless jailer.

What time?

Conseil and I will be at the dinghy at 10 o'clock.

Ned had been secretly stocking the dinghy with food and water.

I'll follow you!

The sea is rough and there's a strong wind blowing, but I'm not afraid of tackling 20 miles in it.

Nearly 10 o'clock. To reach the hatch I had to cross the saloon. It was in darkness, but to my horror the captain was there.

He was seated at the organ, playing a melody of infinite sadness.

He was so absorbed that I might have been invisible. A sob broke from him.

Dear God! Enough! Enough!

These were the last words I heard him say. Were they a cry of remorse?[1]

Ned and Conseil were already unscrewing the bolts of the dinghy when the crew below began shouting in alarm.

The Maelstrom![2] The Maelstrom!

The dreaded Norwegian whirlpool from which no ship escapes! The *Nautilus* struggled like a live thing, her steel creaking. I was rigid with terror. Ned's voice was lost in the roar of the waters.

Screw the bolts down again! If we stay with the *Nautilus* we may be saved.

1. remorse: regret and guilt.
2. Maelstrom: a series of eddies and whirlpools next to the Lofoten Islands, off the north coast of Norway. It has some of the most powerful currents in the world (though Verne's description of it is greatly exaggerated).

Crouched in the dinghy, we felt the *Nautilus* spinning ever faster in smaller and smaller circles. There was a loud cracking sound as the dinghy's bolts were wrenched from their sockets and the little boat was torn from its compartment.

We were hurled into the swirling waters like a stone from a sling.

My head struck a rib[1] of the dinghy and I lost consciousness.

I awoke safe and sound in a fisherman's hut.

A miracle, monsieur!

We were picked up by a Norwegian boat.

But what of Captain Nemo? Is he still alive? Or did he seek destruction in the Maelstrom?

One day the waves may wash his manuscript[2] ashore and we shall learn the truth.

And if he is still wandering the seas, may revenge no longer rule in his fierce heart. And may the scientist in him study in peace.

1. rib: one of the frames that support the hull of a wooden boat from the inside.
2. manuscript: hand-written book.

*The End*

# JULES VERNE (1828–1905)

Jules Verne was a hugely popular French novelist who invented the kind of writing that we now call science fiction. His books described travel through the air and underwater, long before navigable aircraft and practical submarines were invented. He even predicted landings on the moon. In his lifetime his reading public was enormous, and he is now the second most translated novelist of all time – beaten only by British mystery writer Agatha Christie.

*Jules Verne*

## EARLY LIFE

Verne was born in Nantes, in western France, where his father was a lawyer. Nantes was a busy seaport town about 39 miles (65 km) from the mouth of the River Loire. Jules, the eldest of five children, often played with his brother along the river bank near their country home, where the sight of sailing ships coming and going along the river gave him an early thirst for travel and adventure.

There is a story that when he was 11 he got himself accepted as a cabin boy on a vessel bound for the West Indies, but was hauled back home by his angry father before it sailed. His father made him promise that in the future, if he planned any sensational travel, it would be strictly imaginary. The tale may be exaggerated, but the promise was certainly kept.

His second great passion, for technical invention, made an early appearance, too. As a schoolboy he would draw his latest ideas – one was for a steam-powered road vehicle – on the schoolroom blackboard while the teacher

was out of the room. His third love was writing. He was producing stories and poems while still at school, and his ambition was to be a playwright.

## PARIS

Verne's parents had more conventional plans for his future. On leaving school he was sent to Paris to study law, like his father. He got his law degree in 1850, but it was soon clear that he was not interested in a legal career. He refused to take over his father's law practice and threw himself into the musical and theatrical world. He began collaborating on plays and comic pieces, including an operetta (comic opera) called *Blind Man's Buff* which had a mild success. But this was not providing enough to live on, and for three years he supplemented his earnings with a poorly paid job as secretary of the Théâtre Lyrique.

In 1857 he married a young widow with two children. The need to support an instant family forced him to take a steady job as a broker at the Stock Exchange. Uninteresting full-time work did not stop him writing, but he had little success in getting anything published.

## A WINNING TEAM

His luck changed in 1862, through an introduction to the highly successful publisher Pierre-Jules Hetzel. Hetzel thought there were possibilities in a novel which Verne showed him, called "Five Weeks in a Balloon." He suggested several changes to make the story less heavily "educational" and more fun. The rewritten novel became the runaway success of 1863. Verne declared that he had created a novel of a new type, "one all my own." This was true to an extent. With Hetzel's tactful editing, Verne had hit upon a way of combining science and adventure, and of linking them entertainingly to topics in the news – in this case, air travel and African exploration.

This was the beginning of a lifelong partnership between novelist and publisher. Even before the first copies of *Five Weeks in a Balloon* went on sale, Verne was working on the next adventure. He resigned from the Stock Exchange and in 1866 signed a 20-year contract with Hetzel for a minimum of 40 novels in a series to be known as *Voyages Extraordinaires* (Extraordinary

Journeys). By the end of his career he had produced 54 Extraordinary Journeys in which he predicted almost every major technological development of the 20th century, through adventures set in every part of the world.

## SUCCESS

He was now successful enough to buy a town house in Paris, a summer cottage on the River Somme, and a yacht which he treated as his floating study – a masculine retreat in which he wrote many of his books. His voyages to ports around Europe and the Mediterranean provided material for his short stories and novels.

As his books became ever more popular, he became a personality at home and abroad. He bought a much grander yacht and entertained lavishly. He was honored by heads of state and received so many royal invitations that he once upped anchor to avoid meeting the Prince of Wales.

In 1871 Verne and his family settled in Amiens, France, where his later years were no longer spent in a blaze of publicity. He entered local politics and served as a town councilman for 16 years.

Verne's later writing shows a much less optimistic outlook. In 1886 his mentally ill nephew fired two shots at him, wounding him in the leg. This gave him a permanent limp which led to his giving up his much-loved yacht. The death of Hetzel in the next year was a further blow. Verne continued to produce novels without Hetzel's helpful advice until his death in 1905 at the age of 77.

Verne was not himself a trained scientist, but he had a gift for making use of scientific ideas. Through Hetzel he made a wide circle of scientific friends, and much of the research for his books was done through discussing the latest scientific breakthroughs with them. His genius lay in his ability to predict how technology might develop in the future and to combine this vision with first-rate storytelling.

## COMBINING SCIENCE AND FICTION

The meeting with Hetzel was crucial to his success. Before that, publishers had turned down his work as "too scientific." He was so discouraged that he threw his first version of *Five Weeks in a Balloon* onto the fire, but his wife rescued it and encouraged him to keep trying.

Hetzel shared Verne's enthusiasm for popularizing science, and was planning a magazine that would educate and entertain younger readers. He saw that, with certain changes, Verne's work could be exactly what he was looking for. He advised Verne to make his stories more humorous and less political, and avoid any gloomy predictions or unhappy endings. The first issue of Hetzel's *Magazine d'Education et de Récréation* (*Education and Recreation Magazine*) appeared in March 1864; it came out twice a month and had lots of illustrations. Verne's novels became a regular feature of the series. At the end of each year the installments were reprinted in book form for the Christmas market. Verne threw himself into the work with enthusiasm, his imagination taking him right into the imaginary world he was describing. Reporting to Hetzel on his progress on a novel about the North Pole, he wrote: "I'm in the middle of my subject at 80 degrees latitude and 40 degrees centigrade [Celsius] below zero. I'm catching cold just writing about it!"

The partnership turned out one successful novel after another. When *Around the World in Eighty Days* was serialized (published one section at a time in consecutive editions of a publication) in 1873, bets were placed all over the world on the outcome of each chapter. How would its hero, Phileas Fogg, overcome the latest setback in his bid to beat the clock around the globe? From Paris, foreign correspondents of the world's newspapers cabled home a summary of each installment as it appeared.

## WARNINGS OF THE FUTURE

Verne's most popular stories suggest that he was naturally an optimist, confident that science would make the world a better place. But a number of his novels, especially those that appeared after Hetzel's death in 1887, are concerned with the misuse of technology and the harm it can do to the environment. In *The Ice Sphinx* (also called *An Antarctic Mystery*) he predicts the large-scale reduction of whale populations; in *The Begum's Fortune* he warns that technology and scientific knowledge in the hands of evil people can lead to destruction.

Hetzel refused to publish *Paris in the Twentieth Century*, which Verne wrote in 1863, because he thought it too pessimistic for his readers. It describes a world of glass skyscrapers, gas-powered vehicles, high-speed trains, weather control, and instant communication worldwide – yet none of this can make the hero happy, and his life ends in tragedy. Hetzel thought the novel would damage Verne's booming career. He told him to put it away for twenty years. Verne put the manuscript in a safe, where it was discovered by his great-grandson in 1989; it was finally published in 1994.

## VERNE'S LEGACY

Ten unfinished novels were published after Verne's death, though these were heavily edited and sometimes rewritten by his son Michel. They bring his grand total to 64 novels, as well as many short stories and six works of non-fiction.

Here are the English titles of some of his best-known novels:

1863: *Five Weeks in a Balloon*
1864: *The Adventures of Captain Hatteras*
1864: *Journey to the Center of the Earth*
1865: *From the Earth to the Moon*
1867–1868: *In Search of the Castaways*
1869–1870: *20,000 Leagues Under the Sea*
1870: *Around the Moon*
1873: *Around the World in Eighty Days*
1874: *The Mysterious Island*
1876: *Michael Strogoff*
1877: *Off on a Comet*
1879: *The Begum's Fortune*
1897: *The Ice Sphinx (An Antarctic Mystery)*

*Two illustrations from the first edition of* 20,000 Leagues: *the engine room and the giant squid.*

# 20,000 LEAGUES

2 0,000 *Leagues Under the Sea* is probably the best known and best loved of Verne's books today, though *Around the World in Eighty Days* was a bigger success at the time of publication. The title needs some explaining. 20,000 leagues is the distance covered by the captives aboard the *Nautilus*, not the depth at which they travelled. The French league in Verne's day was calculated to be 2.5 miles (4 km), so Professor Aronnax had 50,000 miles of happy underwater study, while Ned Land had 50,000 miles of claustrophobia and agonizing boredom.

### VERNE AND THE SEA

It may have been Verne's first long sea voyage, to America in 1867, that inspired him to write a novel in praise of the wonders of the sea. Like most of his books, it appeared in serial form at first, and to keep his readers in suspense he was careful to provide a good plot twist in each installment. But interleaved with the exciting episodes are long passages of description and information which modern readers may find heavy going.

Today we like to pick up knowledge here and there, from films, television, the Internet, etc.; we don't expect to work at it. But in the 19th century people were quite prepared to read a lot of facts. Verne wanted his book to teach people the wonders of marine science, as well as telling them a good story. So he makes Aronnax explain all sorts of things to the patiently listening Conseil, including the origin of pearls, the nature of sponges, and the movements of the Gulf Stream. The astounding underwater scenery that entrances Aronnax is a prodigious feat of Verne's imagination, for in the days before underwater photography no one had ever seen such a world. Purely through his mind's eye, Verne was able to picture the various habitats of the world's oceans and describe their species at encyclopedic length.

### PREDICTING THE FUTURE

Verne was so accurate in his predictions that many of the wonders he describes have become commonplace. Today's readers must put on 19th-century spectacles to understand how amazing his ideas were. A vessel capable of travelling at great speed underwater and staying submerged for long periods was an impossibility when Verne wrote. (Some experimental man-powered submarines had been built, but they were small, slow, fragile, and very dangerous to travel in.) The notion that electricity could provide enough power to drive engines and to light and heat rooms seemed equally far-fetched (though electric light and power would become a reality in Verne's lifetime). Neither the North or South Poles had been reached, but Verne was right in thinking polar travel would be possible under the ice cap (though in reality this is only possible at the North Pole – the South Pole is on dry land). In 1958 a US submarine was the first naval vessel to reach the North Pole. Appropriately, it was named the *Nautilus*!

## WHO IS CAPTAIN NEMO?

Despite its heavy blocks of information the book remains a favorite, and this is undoubtedly due to the appeal of its enigmatic hero/villain Captain Nemo.

In *20,000 Leagues* we never learn his true identity (Nemo means "nobody" in Latin), or why he is seeking revenge. Verne originally meant him to be a Polish nobleman who had lost his wife and children in the Polish patriotic "January Uprising" of 1863, in which thousands of Poles had been killed or deported to Siberia by the Russians. Hetzel took fright at this. Russia was an ally of France, so he thought it would cause offense and they would lose readers. He made Verne cut out the explanation, thereby adding to the air of mystery around the Captain.

But Nemo has a life of his own. He crops up today in various guises and in all sorts of new adventures, in films, comic strips, and even pop songs. Verne could not resist reviving him. He reappears (having survived the Maelstrom) in Verne's 1874 novel *The Mysterious Island*, where it is revealed that he is an Indian, Prince Dakkar, son of the Rajah of Bundelkund. Because of the prince's leading role in the Sepoy Revolt against the British Empire in 1857, his family and kingdom had been destroyed by the British, who put a price on his head. Britain and France were traditional enemies, so Hetzel was not afraid of upsetting British readers!

*Nemo observing the position of the sun: an illustration from the first edition of* 20,000 Leagues.

## FILMS AND TELEVISION

There have been several film versions of *20,000 Leagues*, though few of them stick closely to the book. An American silent movie was made in 1916, with groundbreaking underwater photography. Walt Disney's 1954 version has James Mason as a dark and commanding Captain Nemo who could have stepped straight out of the book, though Ned Land's song and dance routine could not. The film won an Oscar for its special effects, which included a mechanically operated giant squid. There have been several TV versions; Michael Caine starred in one in 1997. In 2007 the story was updated to modern times, with cutting-edge technology, in a film called *30,000 Leagues Under the Sea*.

## SUBMARINES AND POLAR EXPLORATION

**1620s**
Dutch inventor Cornelis Drebbel demonstrates a submarine in the River Thames in London. It is made of wood and leather, and propelled by oars.

**1775**
American inventor David Bushnell builds an egg-shaped submarine called the *Turtle*, designed to plant mines on the hulls of enemy ships. It is driven by a propeller that is cranked by hand.

**1800**
Robert Fulton, an American living in France, builds a hand-cranked submarine which uses a sail when travelling on the surface. He calls it the *Nautilus*.

**1841**
British naval officer Sir James Clark Ross discovers the Ross Ice Shelf in Antarctica.

**1862**
Both sides in the American Civil War build submarines with hand-cranked propellers: the USS *Alligator* and the CSS *Pioneer*.

**1863**
The French *Plongeur* ("Diver") is the first submarine powered by an engine. It runs on compressed air.

**1864**
February 17: The Confederate Navy's *H. L. Hunley* becomes the first submarine ever to sink an enemy warship. The *Hunley* sinks on its way back to port and none of its crew survive.

**1867**
The Spanish submarine *Ictíneo II*, originally human-powered, is rebuilt to become the first submarine powered by a steam engine. Its name means "fish-ship" in Greek.

**1869–1870**
*20,000 Leagues Under the Sea* is first published in serial form.

**1879**
British clergyman George Garrett builds *Resurgam II*, a steam-powered submarine. Though successful in tests, it sinks before entering service with the Royal Navy. *Resurgam* is Latin for "I shall rise again."

**1886**
Garrett's firm builds the *Abdulhamid* for the Turkish navy – the first submarine ever to fire a torpedo underwater.

**1888**
Spanish engineer Isaac Peral builds an electric submarine. The French *Gymnote*, also electrically powered, is launched only two weeks later.

**1901**
The British Royal Navy receives its first submarine, HMS *Holland 1*.

**1906**
Norwegian explorer Roald Amundsen is the first to complete the Northwest Passage – the journey from the Atlantic to the Pacific via the Arctic Ocean.

**1909**
American explorer Robert Peary claims to have reached the North Pole.

**1911**
December 14: Roald Amundsen is the first to reach the South Pole.

**1912**
January 17: British explorer Robert Falcon Scott reaches the South Pole, but dies on the return journey.

**1926**
May 12: Amundsen flies over the North Pole in an airship – the first confirmed sighting of the Pole.

**1958**
August 3: American submarine USS *Nautilus* crosses the North Pole beneath the ice cap.

# THE VOYAGE OF THE *NAUTILUS*

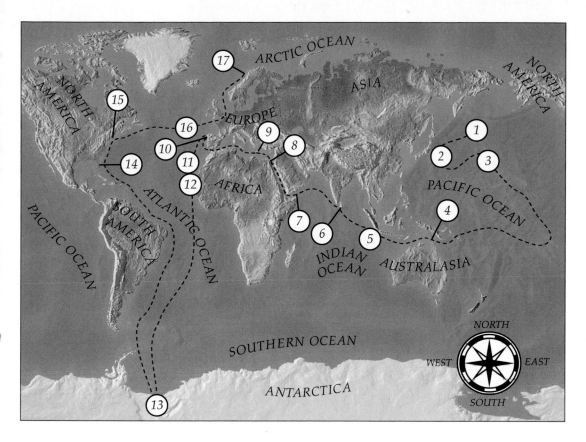

## KEY TO THE MAP

1. A "sea monster" (really the *Nautilus*) is sighted in the North Pacific.
2. *Nautilus* attacks the *Abraham Lincoln* off the coast of Japan; Aronnax, Conseil, and Ned Land become Nemo's prisoners.
3. They hunt in the forests of Crespo.
4. *Nautilus* runs aground in the Torres Strait.
5. A crewman is buried in the coral cemetery.
6. They visit the pearl fisheries of Ceylon (Sri Lanka).
7. They enter the Red Sea.
8. They pass through the Arabian Tunnel into the Mediterranean Sea.
9. Nemo's crewmen deliver gold bars to revolutionaries on Crete.
10. They collect sunken treasure in Vigo Bay, northwest Spain.
11. They visit the ruins of Atlantis.
12. They explore inside the volcano, where Nemo obtains his fuel.
13. They discover the South Pole (which in real life is on the continent of Antarctica, not at sea) and become trapped beneath the ice shelf.
14. The Bahamas: attack of the giant squid.
15. Long Island, New York: Nemo braves the hurricane.
16. *Nautilus* rams and sinks the warship.
17. Lofoten Islands, Norway: *Nautilus* enters the Maelstrom.

# INDEX

IF YOU LIKED THIS BOOK, YOU MIGHT ALSO WANT TO TRY THESE TITLES IN THE BARRON'S *GRAPHIC CLASSICS* SERIES:

*Adventures of Huckleberry Finn*

*Dr. Jekyll and Mr. Hyde*

*Dracula*

*Frankenstein*

*Gulliver's Travels*

*Hamlet*

*The Hunchback of Notre Dame*

*Jane Eyre*

*Journey to the Center of the Earth*

*Julius Caesar*

*Kidnapped*

*Macbeth*

*The Man in the Iron Mask*

*Moby Dick*

*The Odyssey*

*Oliver Twist*

*Romeo & Juliet*

*A Tale of Two Cities*

*The Three Musketeers*

*Treasure Island*

*Wuthering Heights*